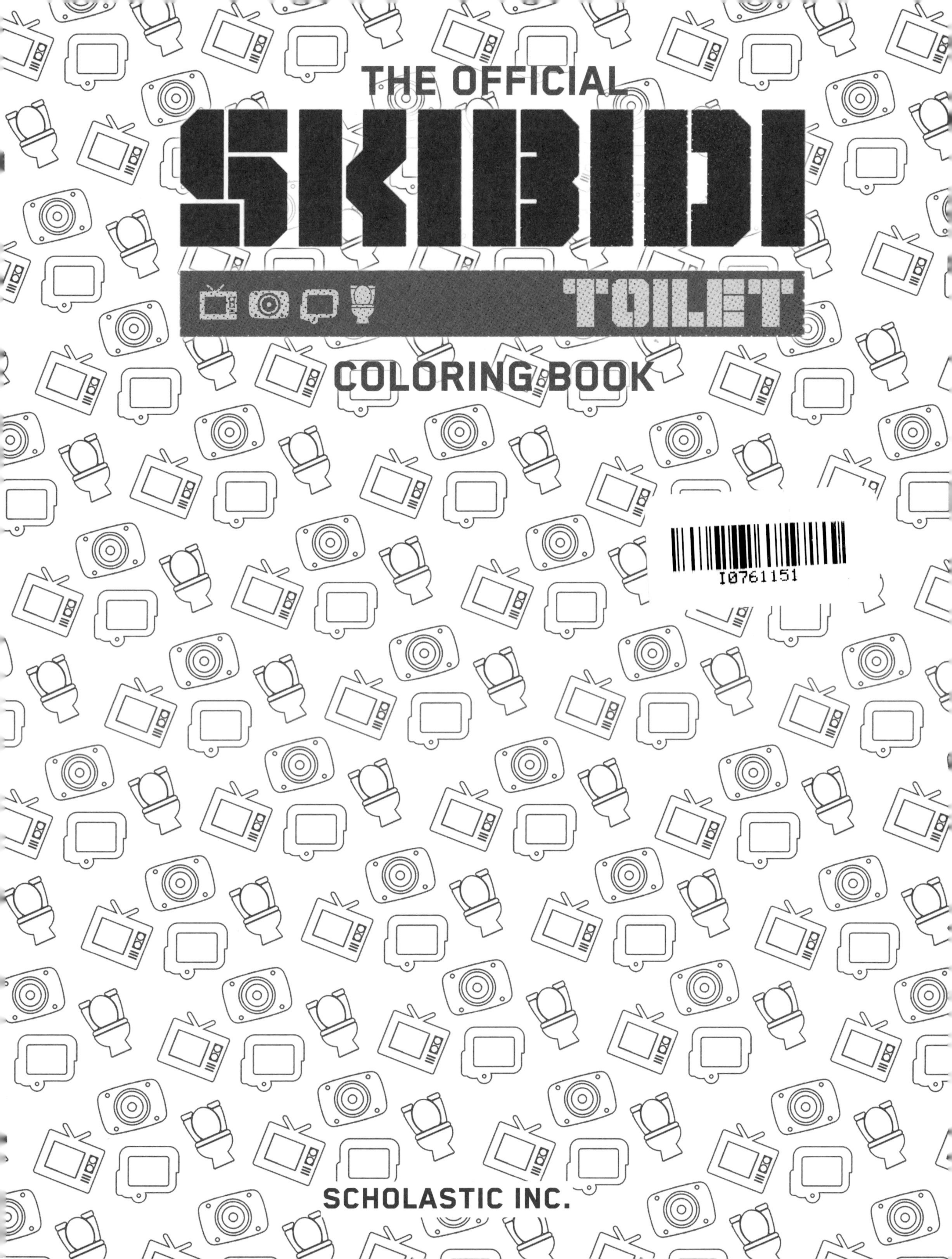
THE OFFICIAL
SKIBIDI
TOILET
COLORING BOOK
I0761151
SCHOLASTIC INC.

SKIBIDI TOILET is a trademark of Invisible Narratives, LLC.
© 2025 Invisible Narratives, LLC. All rights reserved.

All rights reserved. Published by Scholastic Inc., *Publishers since 1920*.
SCHOLASTIC and associated logos are trademarks and/or registered trademarks of Scholastic Inc.

The publisher does not have any control over and does not assume any responsibility for author or third-party websites or their content.

No part of this publication may be reproduced, stored in a retrieval system, or transmitted in any form or by any means, electronic, mechanical, photocopying, recording, or otherwise, or used to train any artificial intelligence technologies, without written permission of the publisher. For information regarding permission, write to Scholastic Inc., Attention: Permissions Department, 557 Broadway, New York, NY 10012.

This book is a work of fiction. Names, characters, places, and incidents are either the product of the author's imagination or are used fictitiously, and any resemblance to actual persons, living or dead, business establishments, events, or locales is entirely coincidental.

ISBN 979-8-225-01235-9

10 9 8 7 6 5 4 3 2 1 25 26 27 28 29

Printed in the U.S.A. 40

First printing 2025

Book design by Martha Maynard and Elliane Mellet

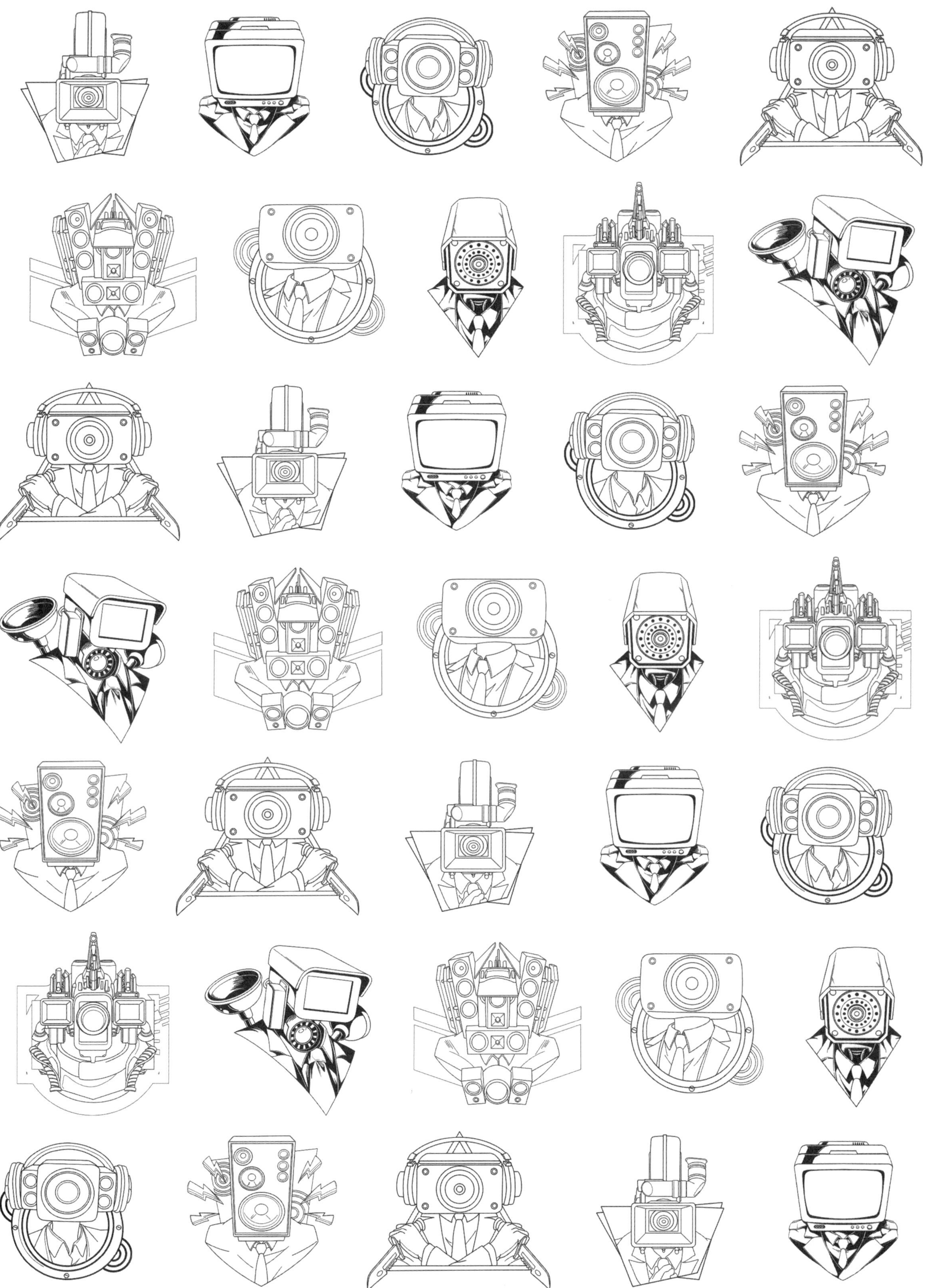

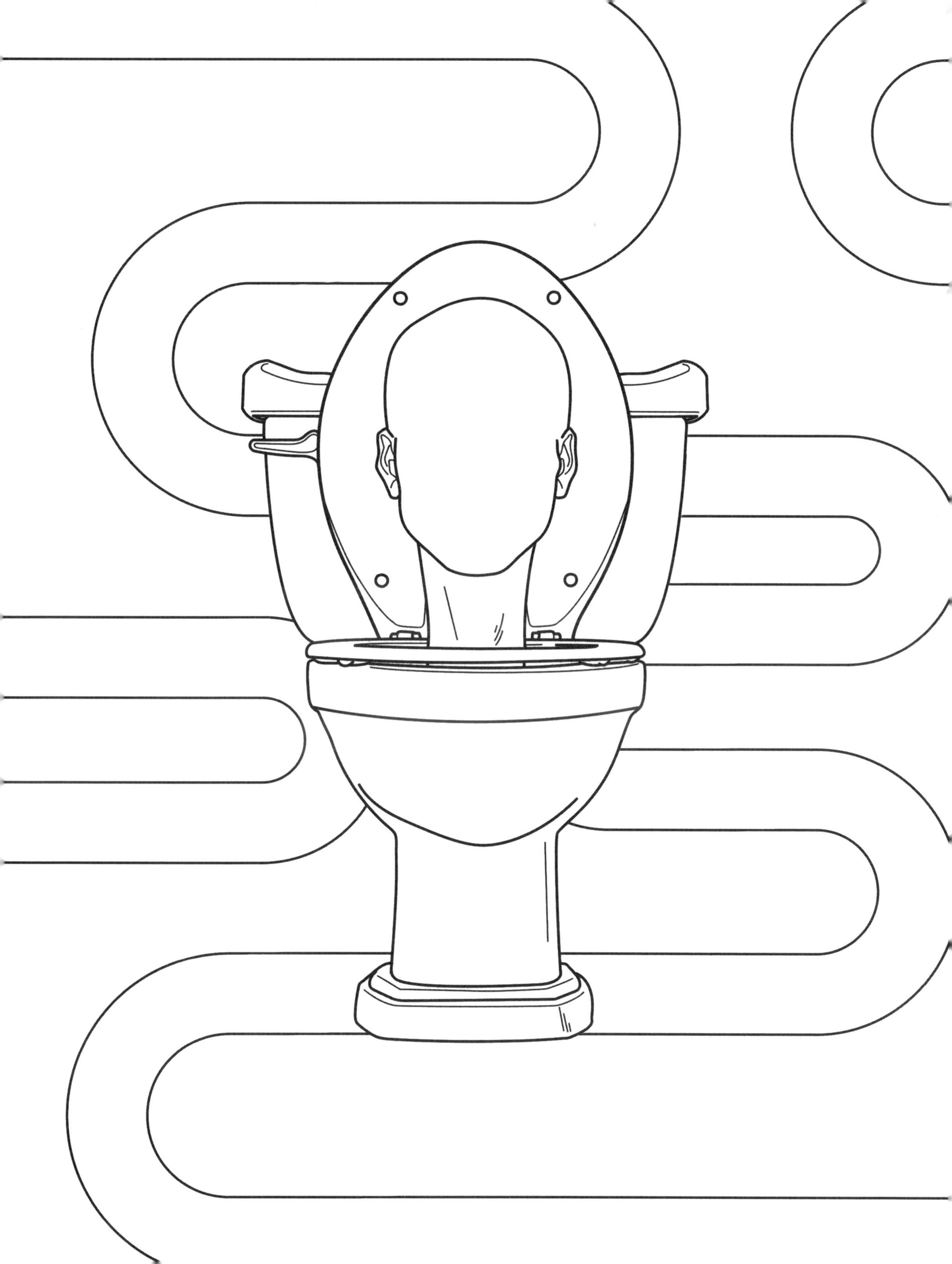

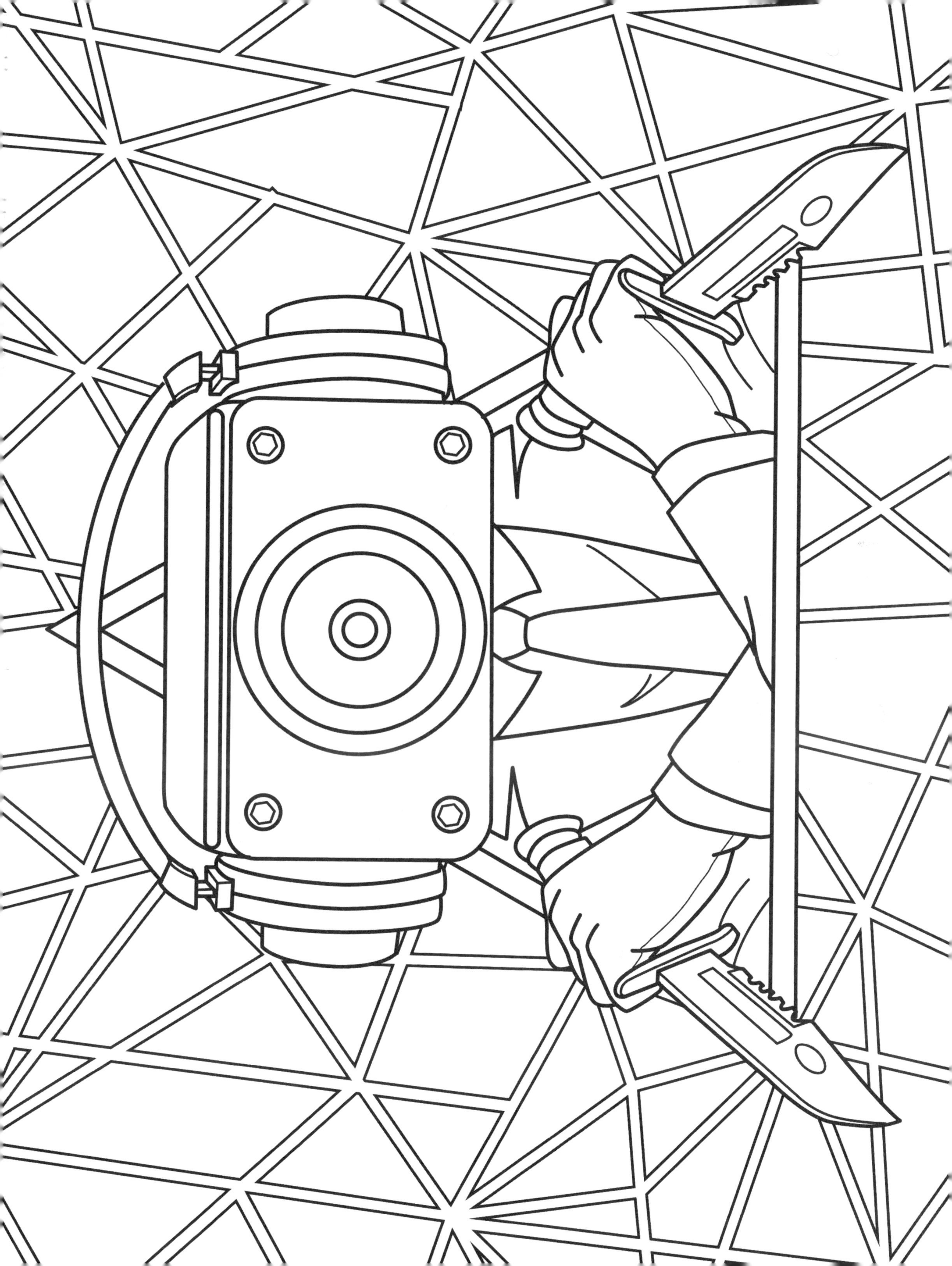

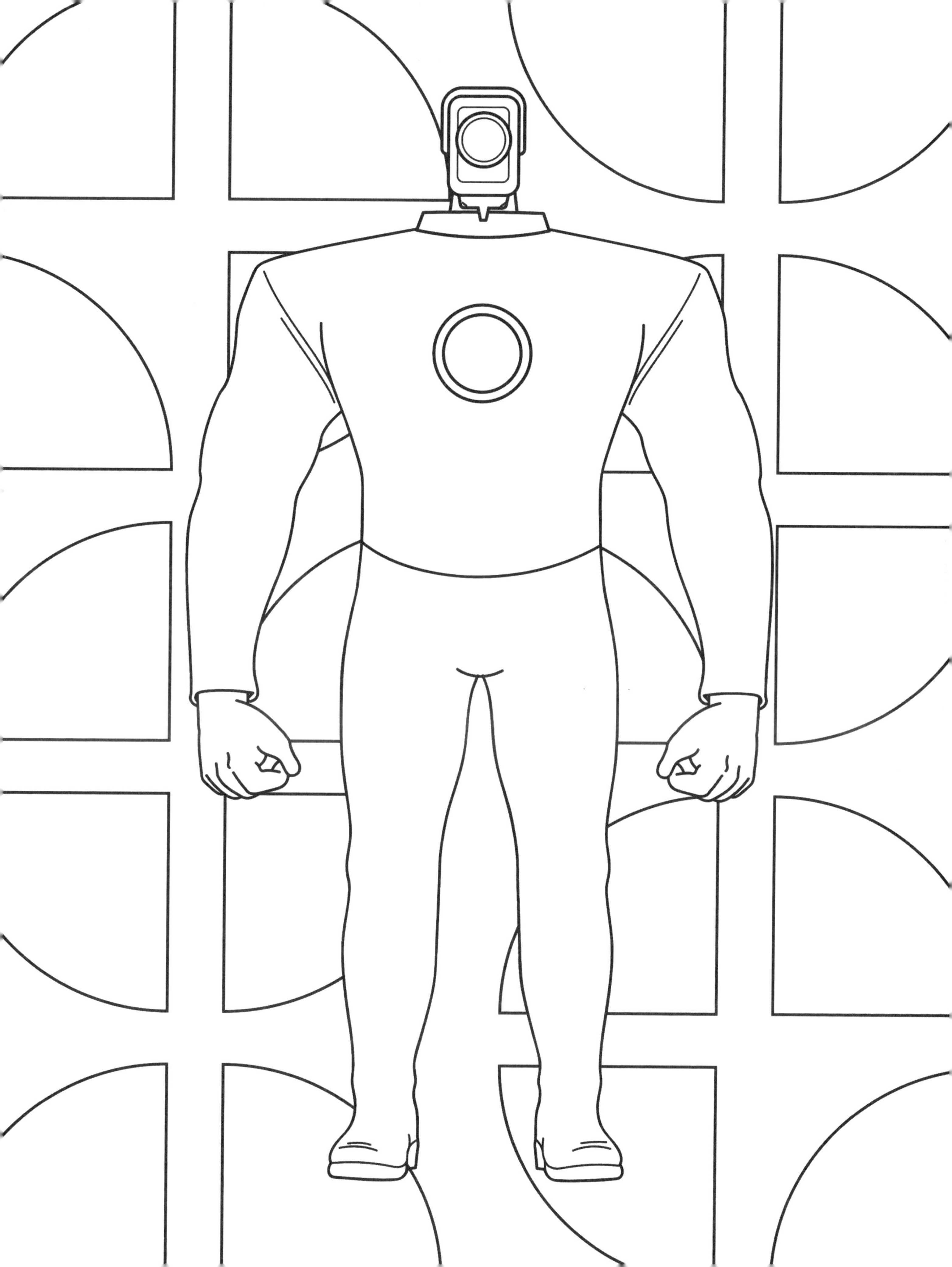

ALL TOILETS
WILL DIE
ALL TOILETS
WILL DIE
ALL TOILETS
WILL DIE

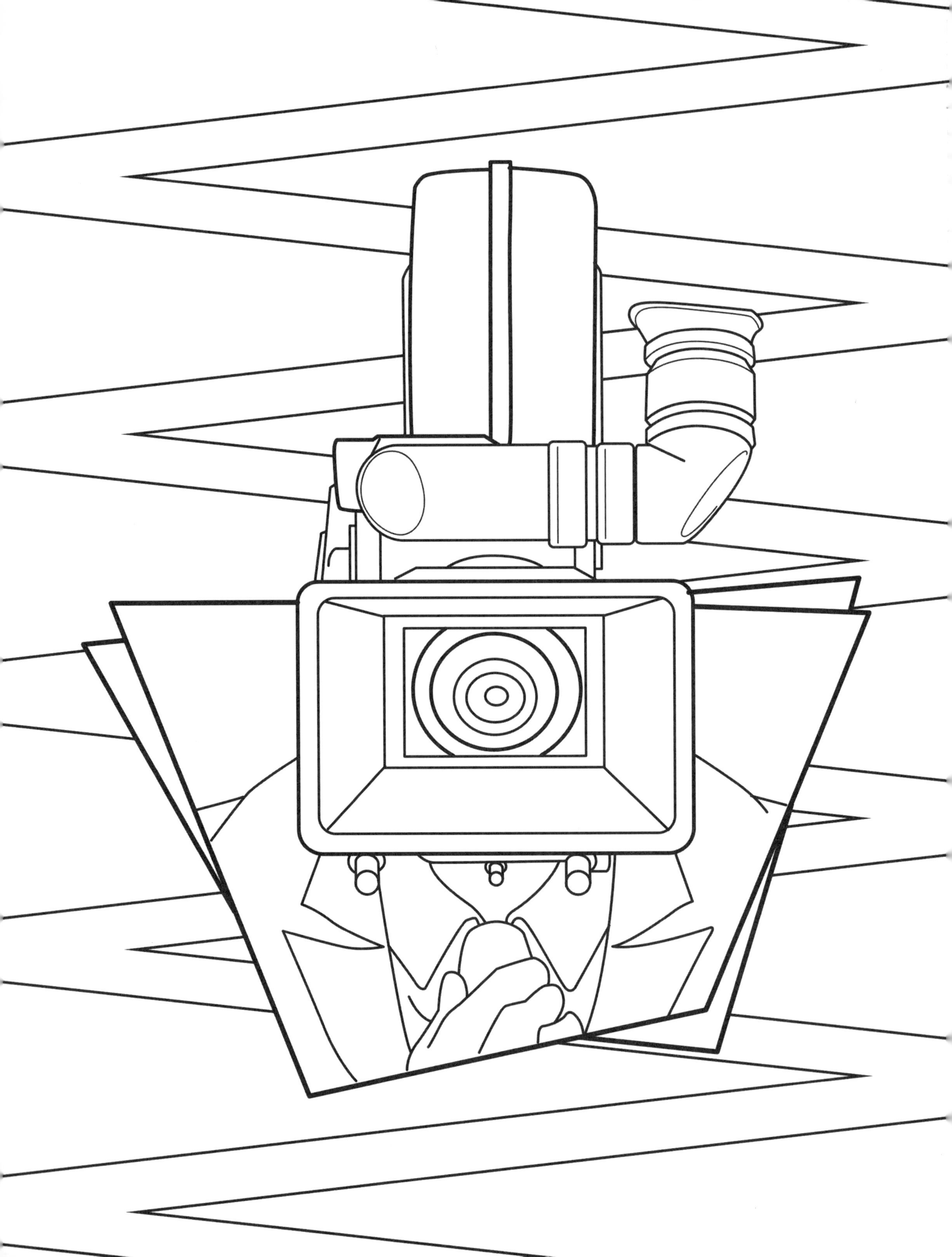

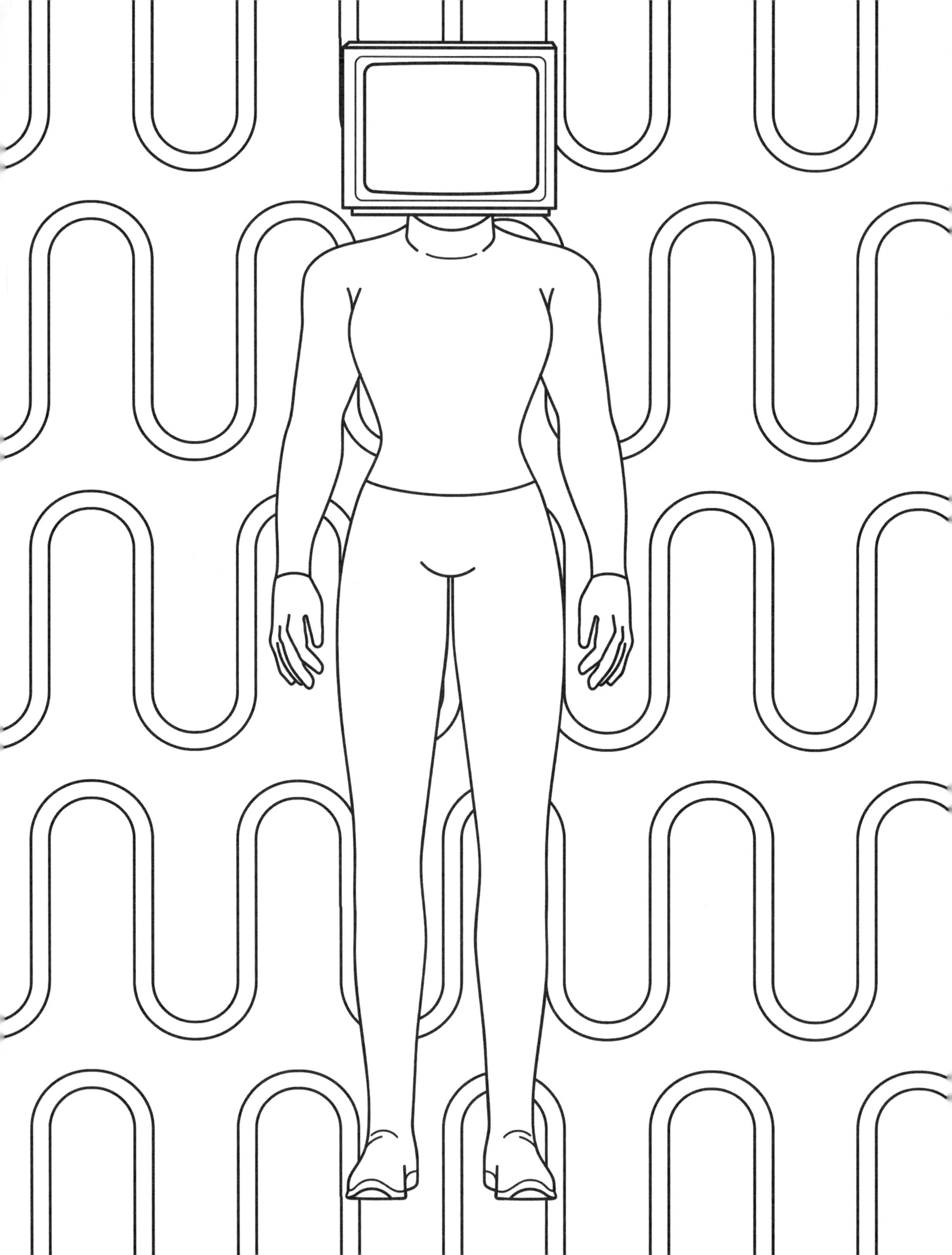

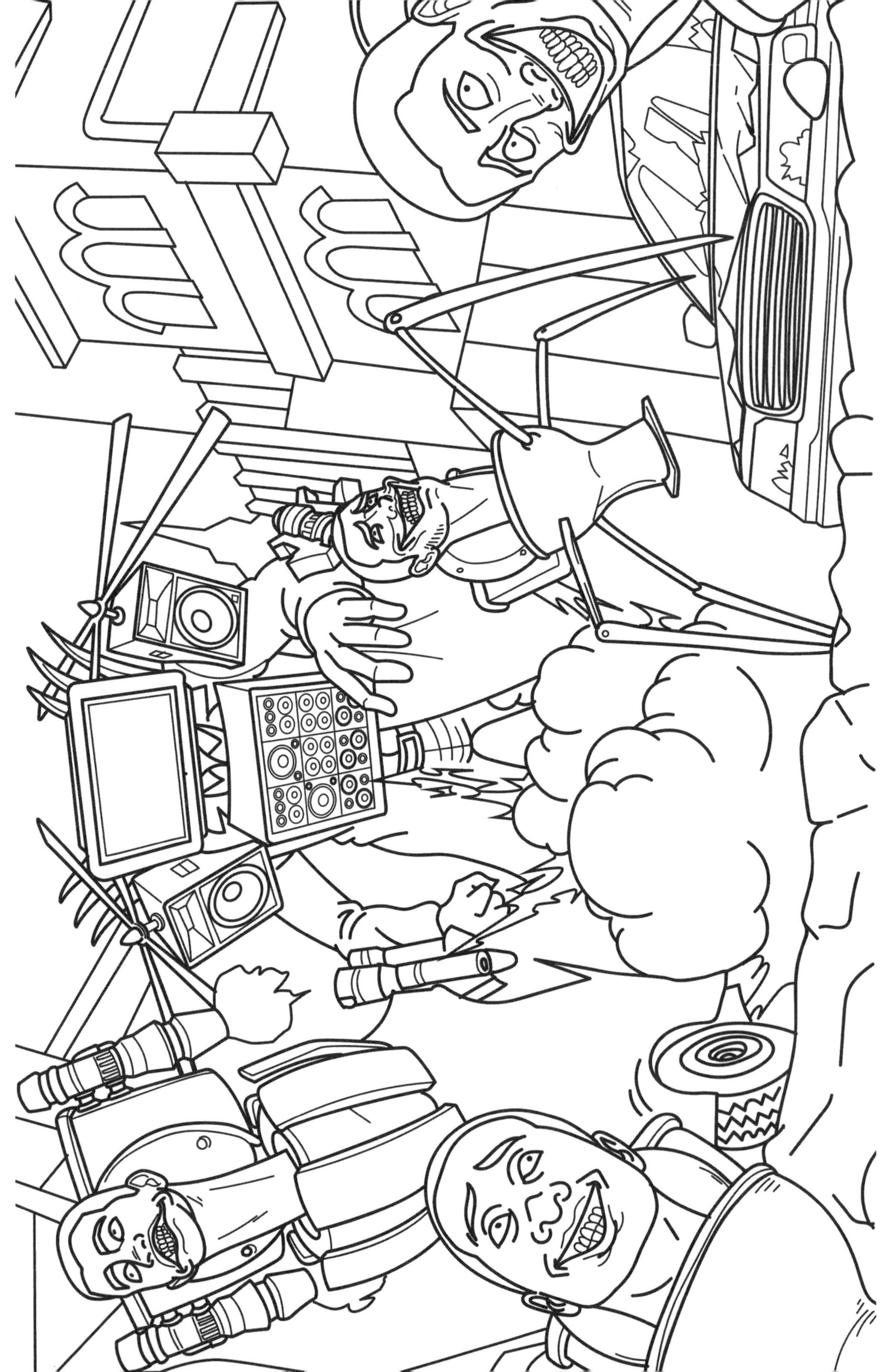

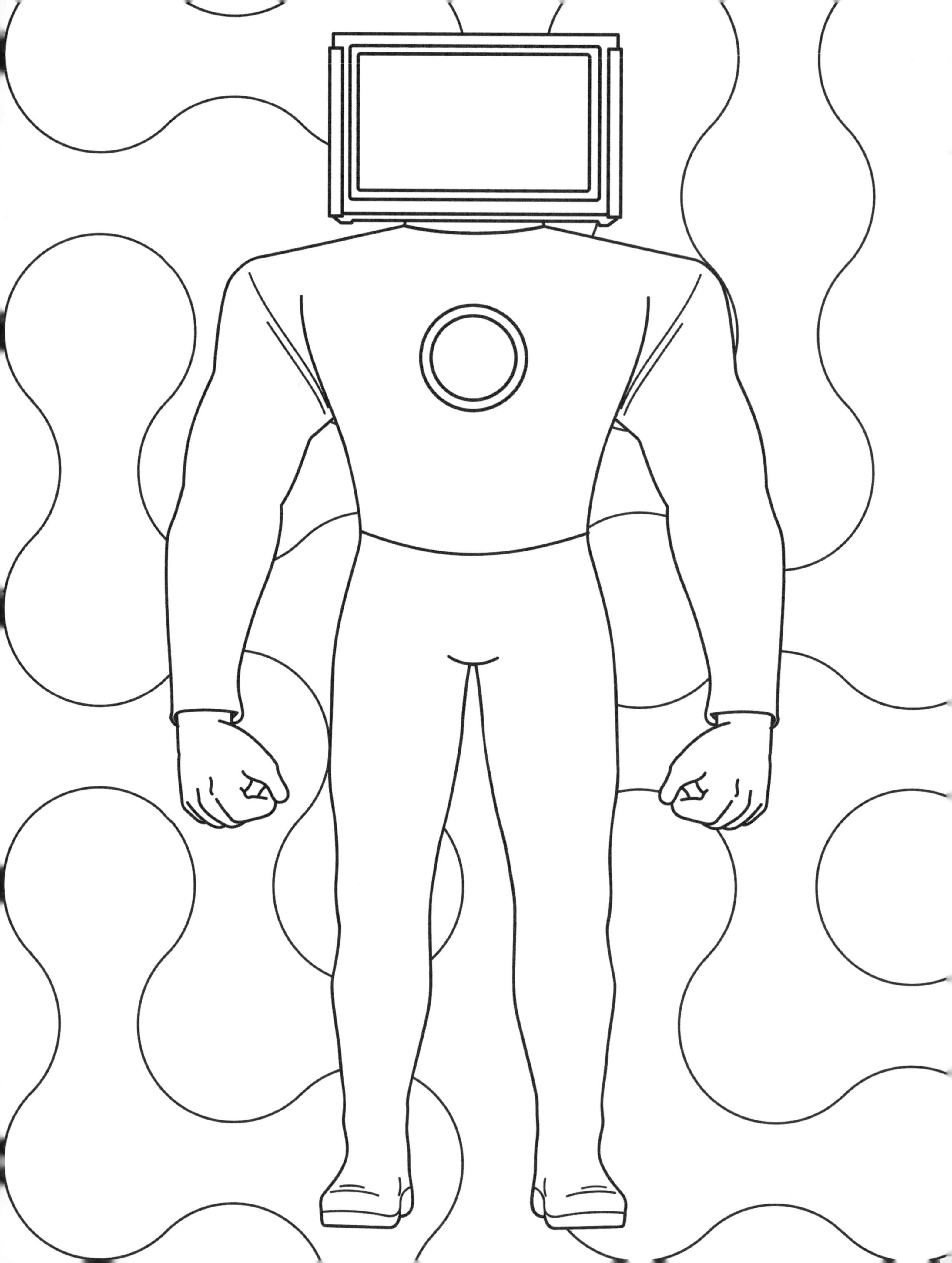

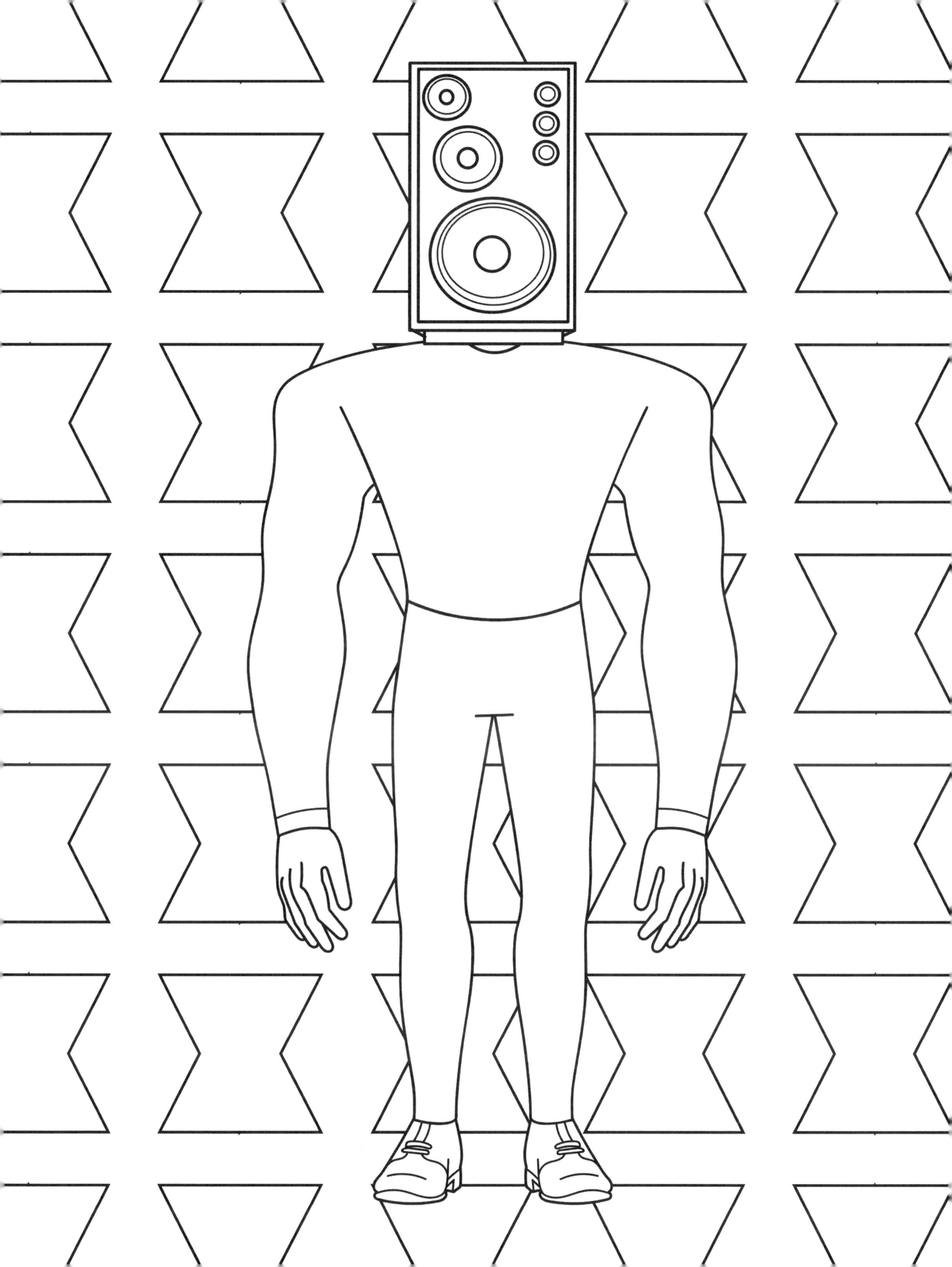

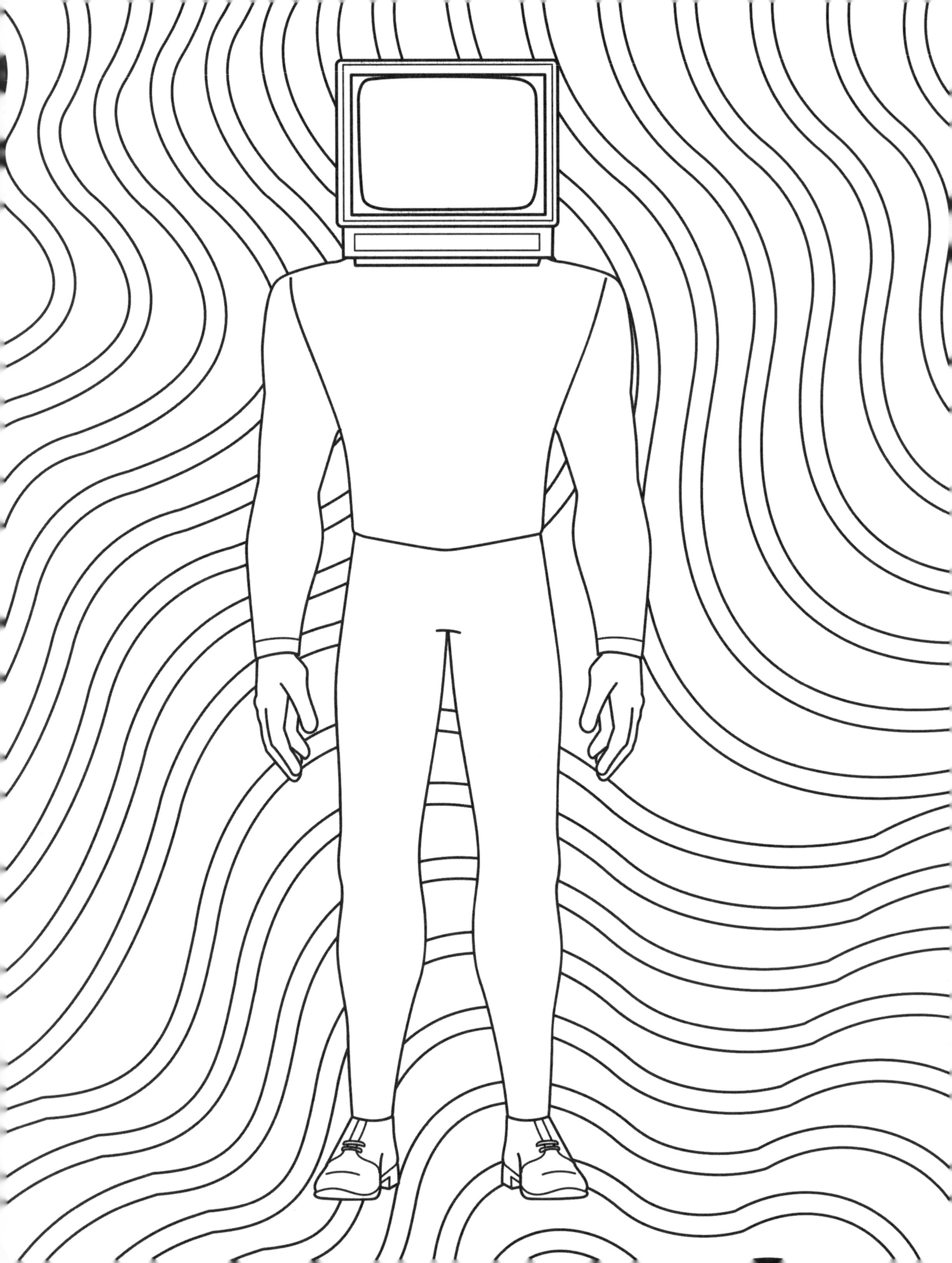

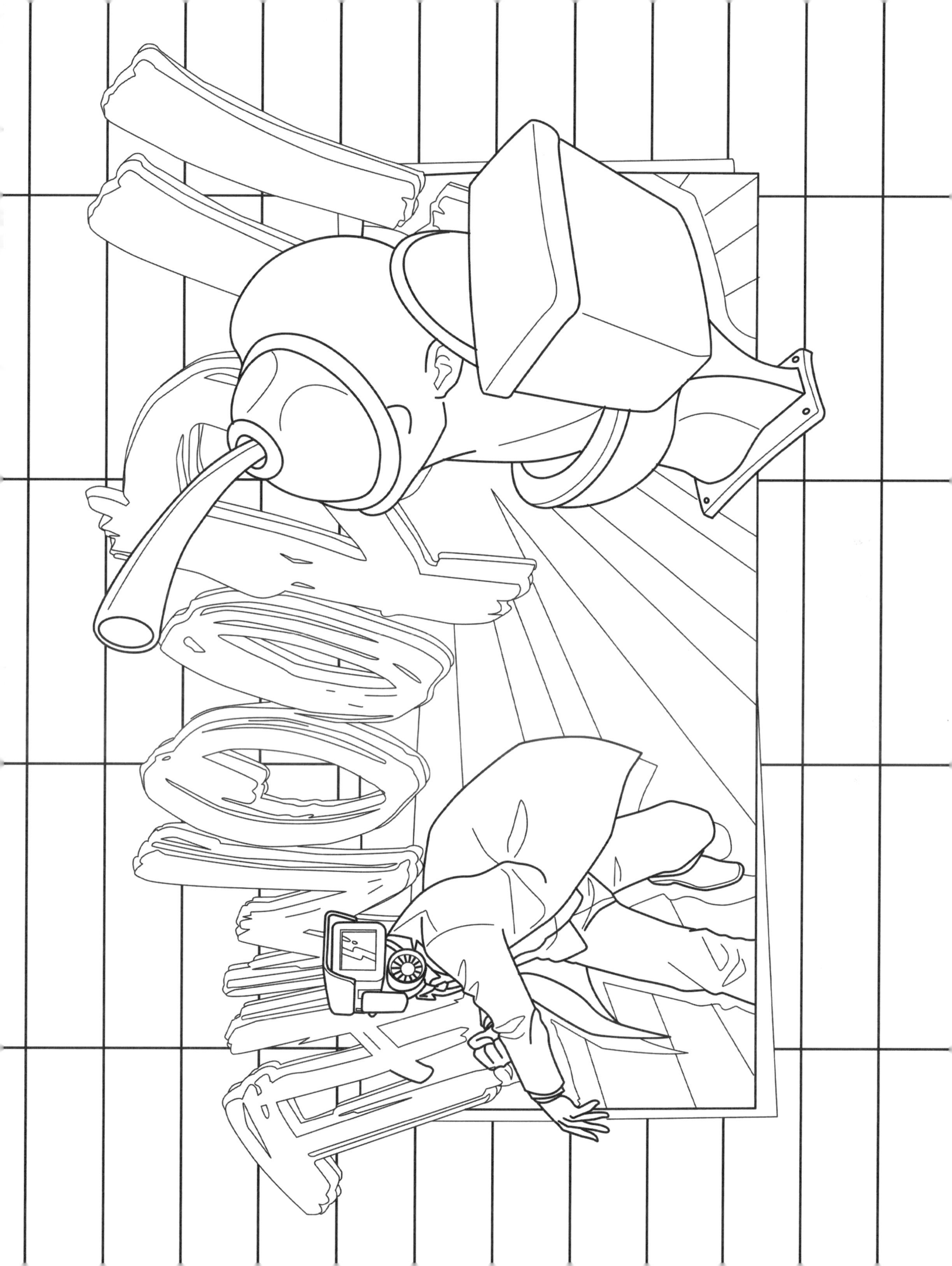

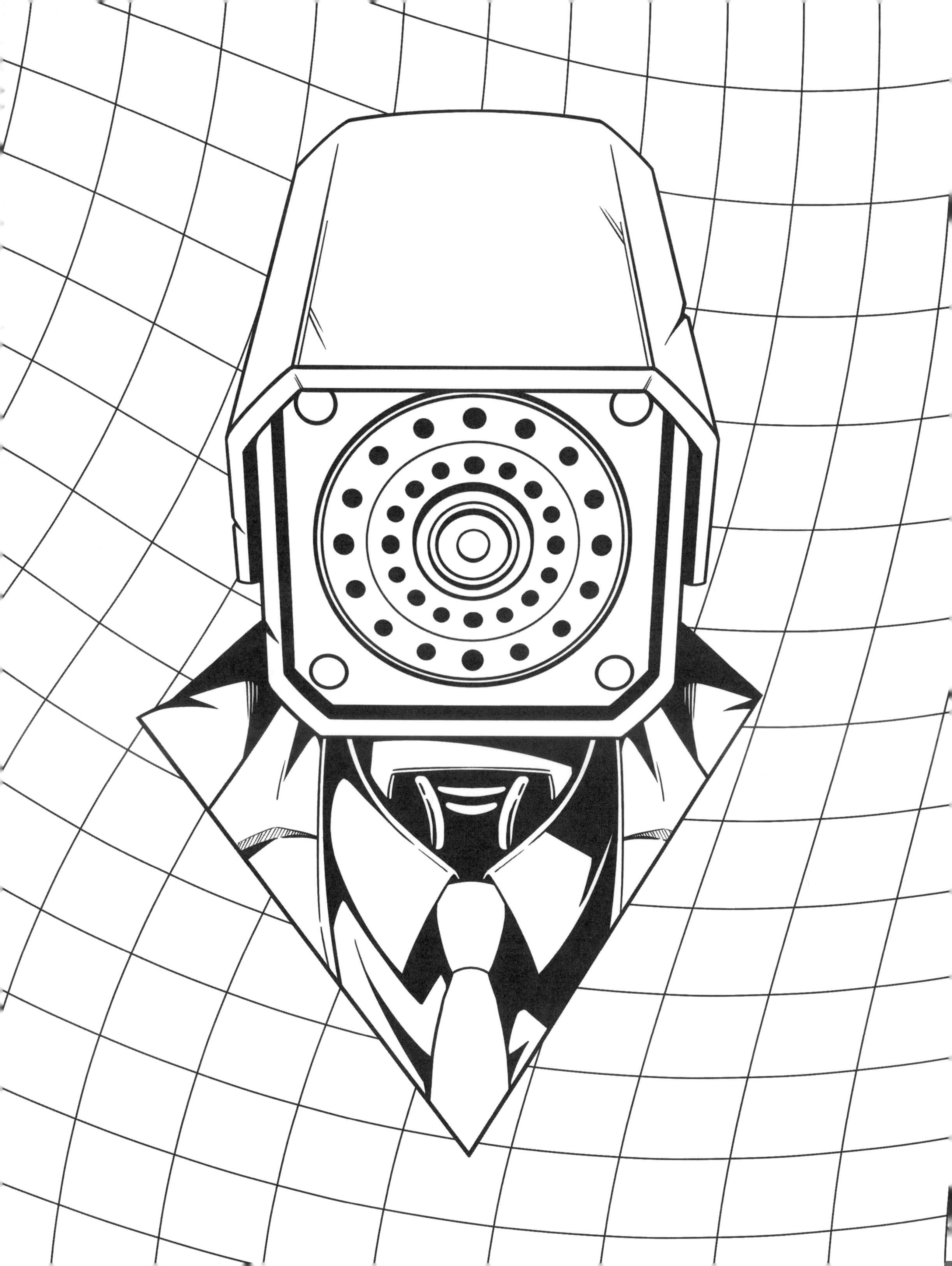

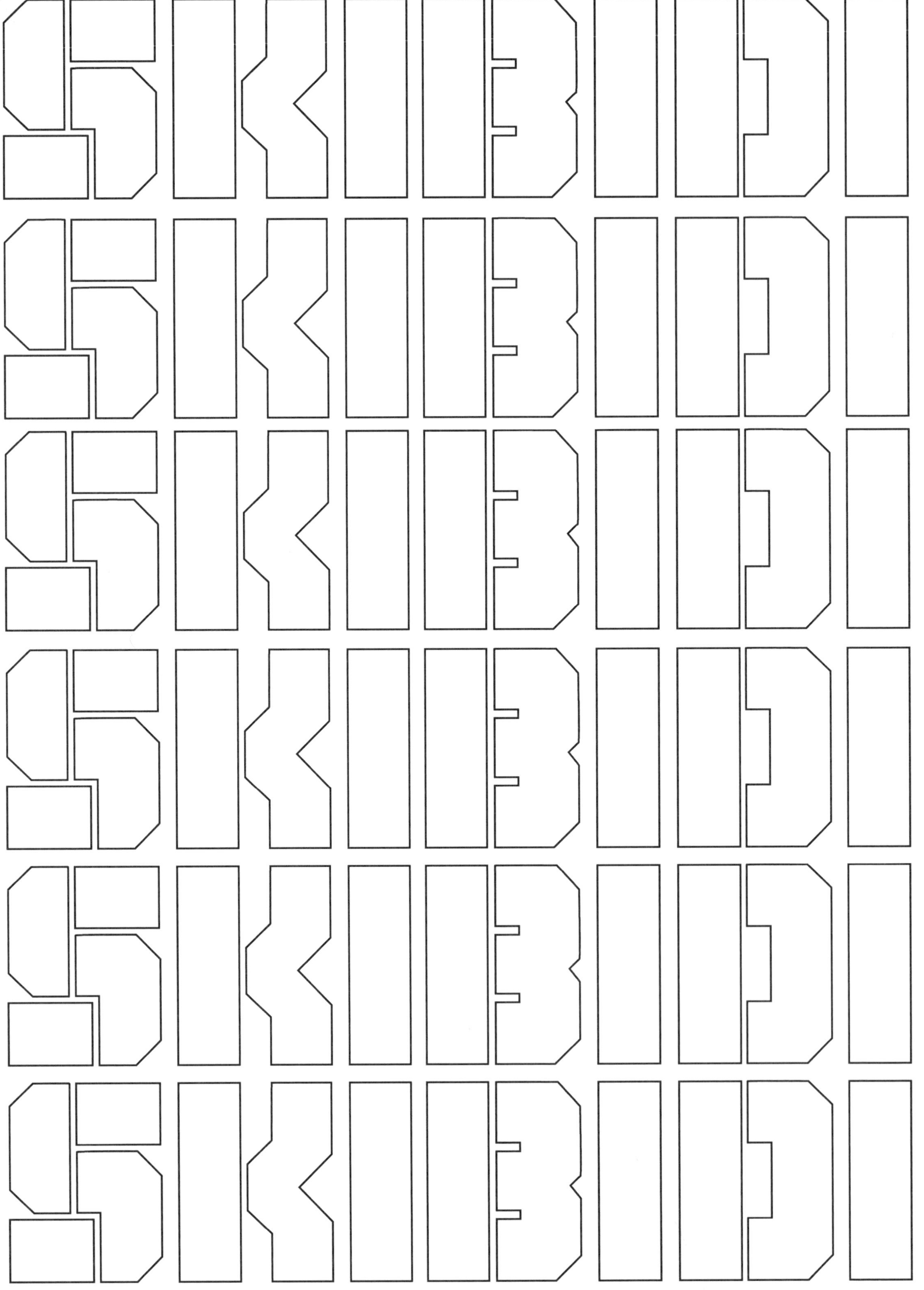
SKIBIDI
SKIBIDI
SKIBIDI
SKIBIDI
SKIBIDI
SKIBIDI

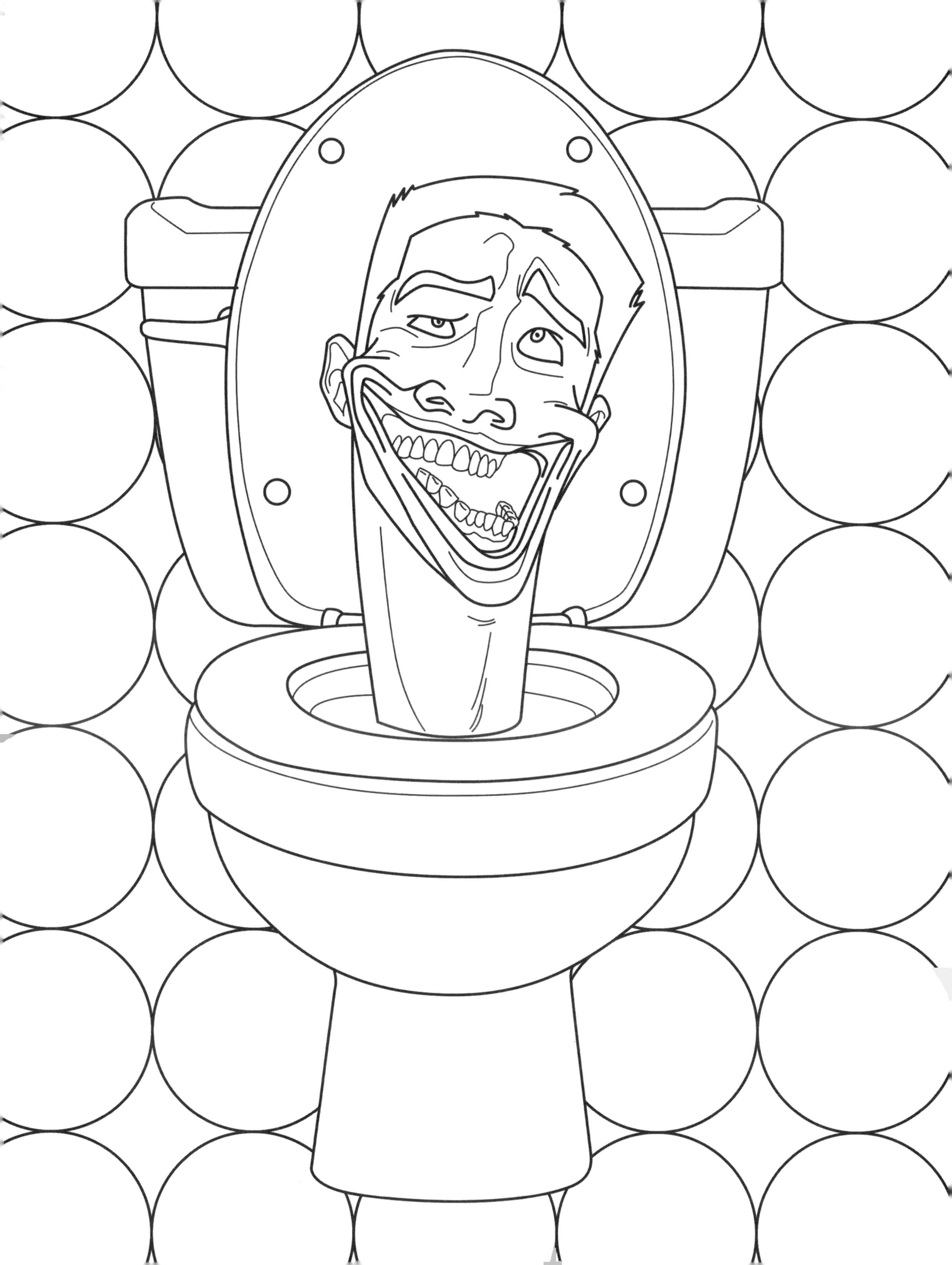

ALL TOILETS
WILL DIE

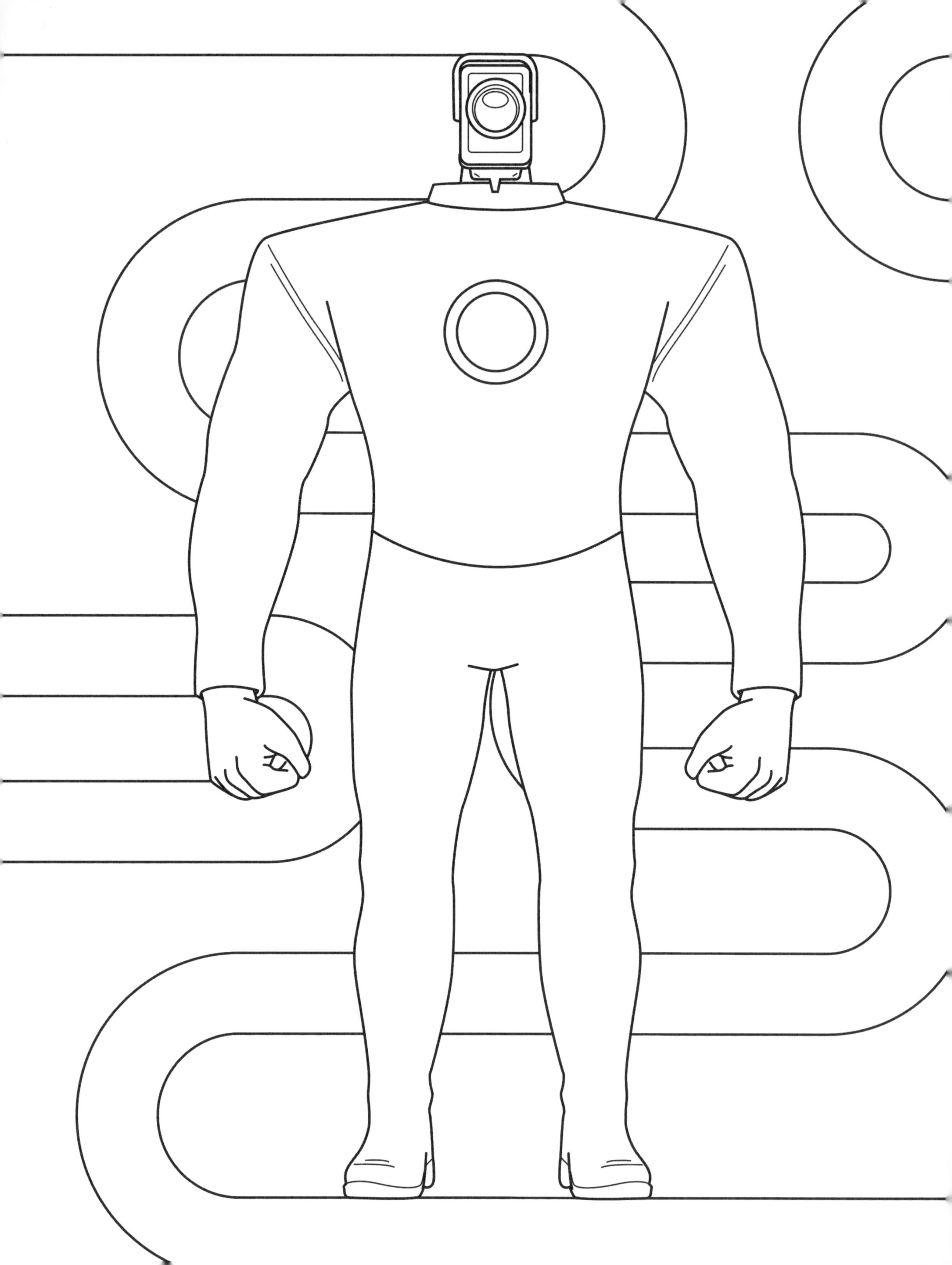

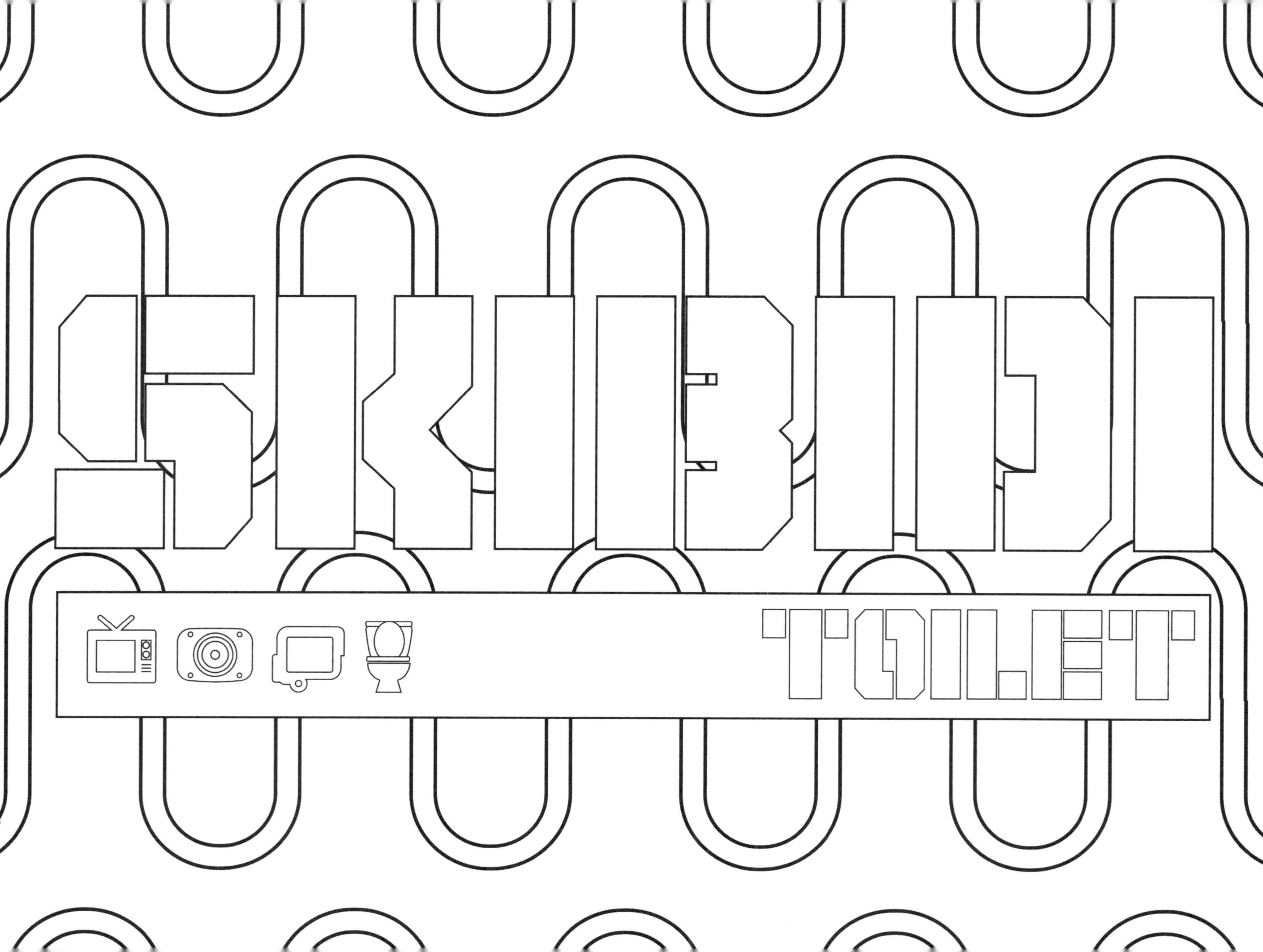
SKIBIDI
TOILET

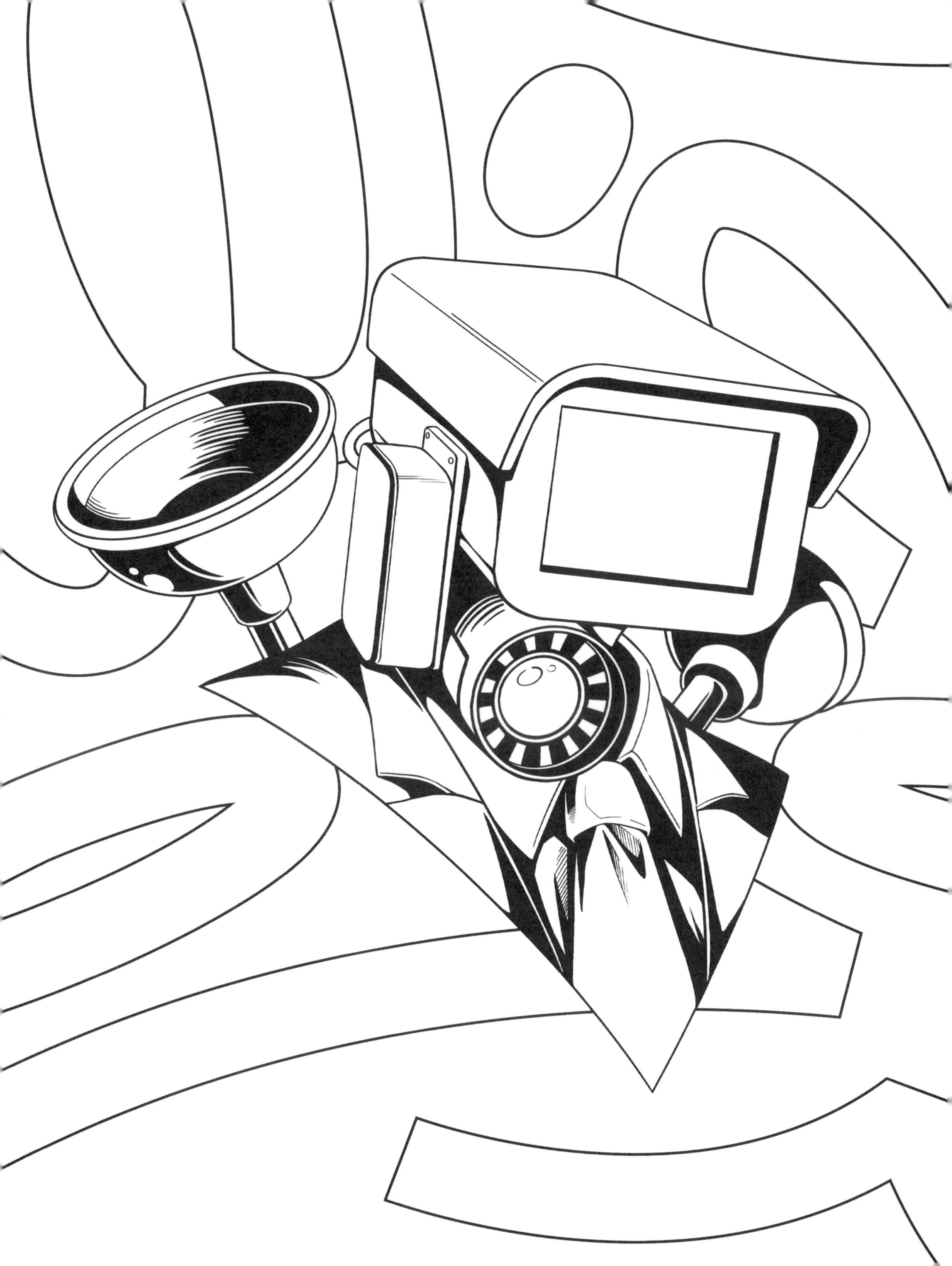

PLUNGERMAN

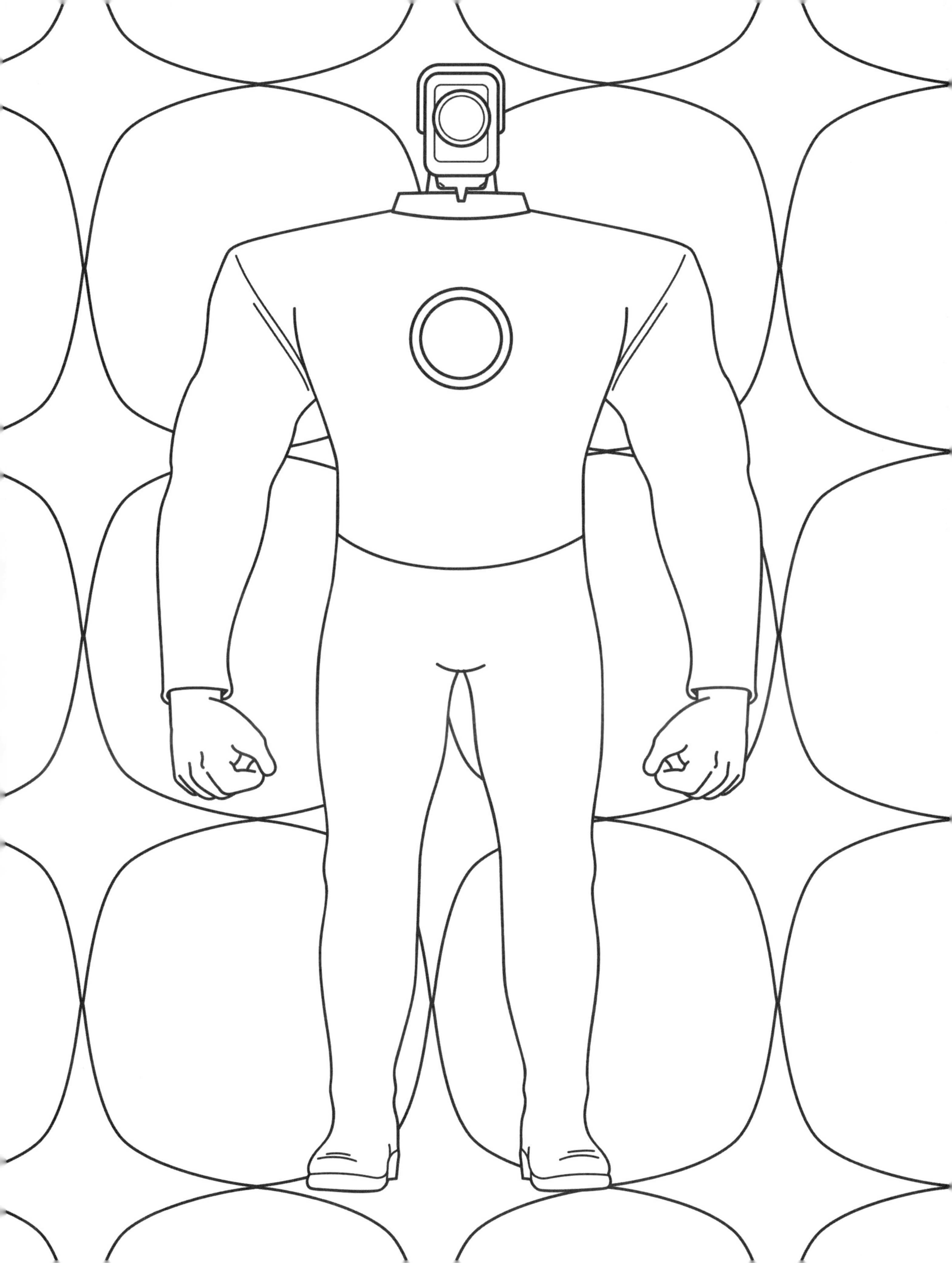

SKIBIDI
TOILET

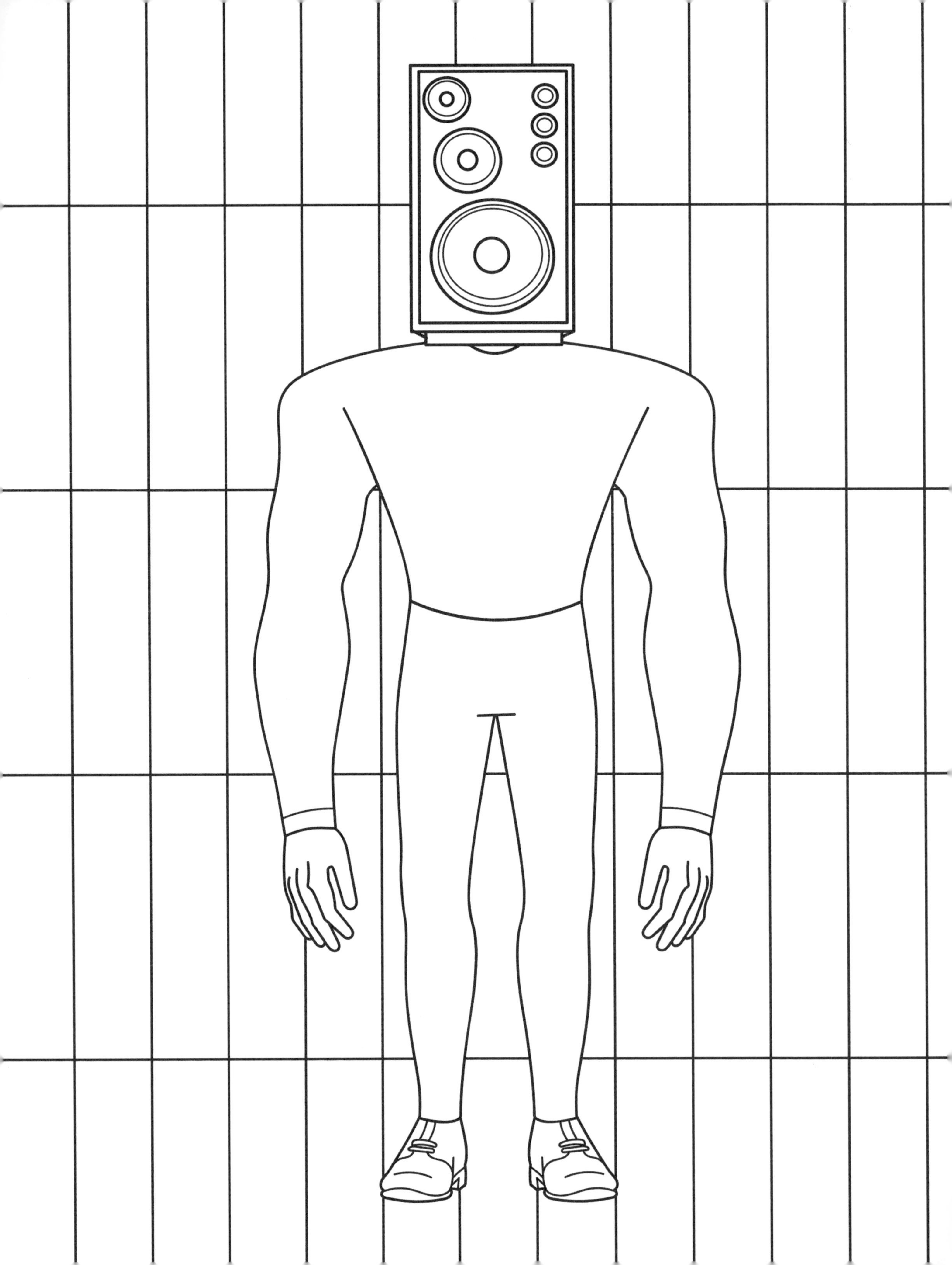

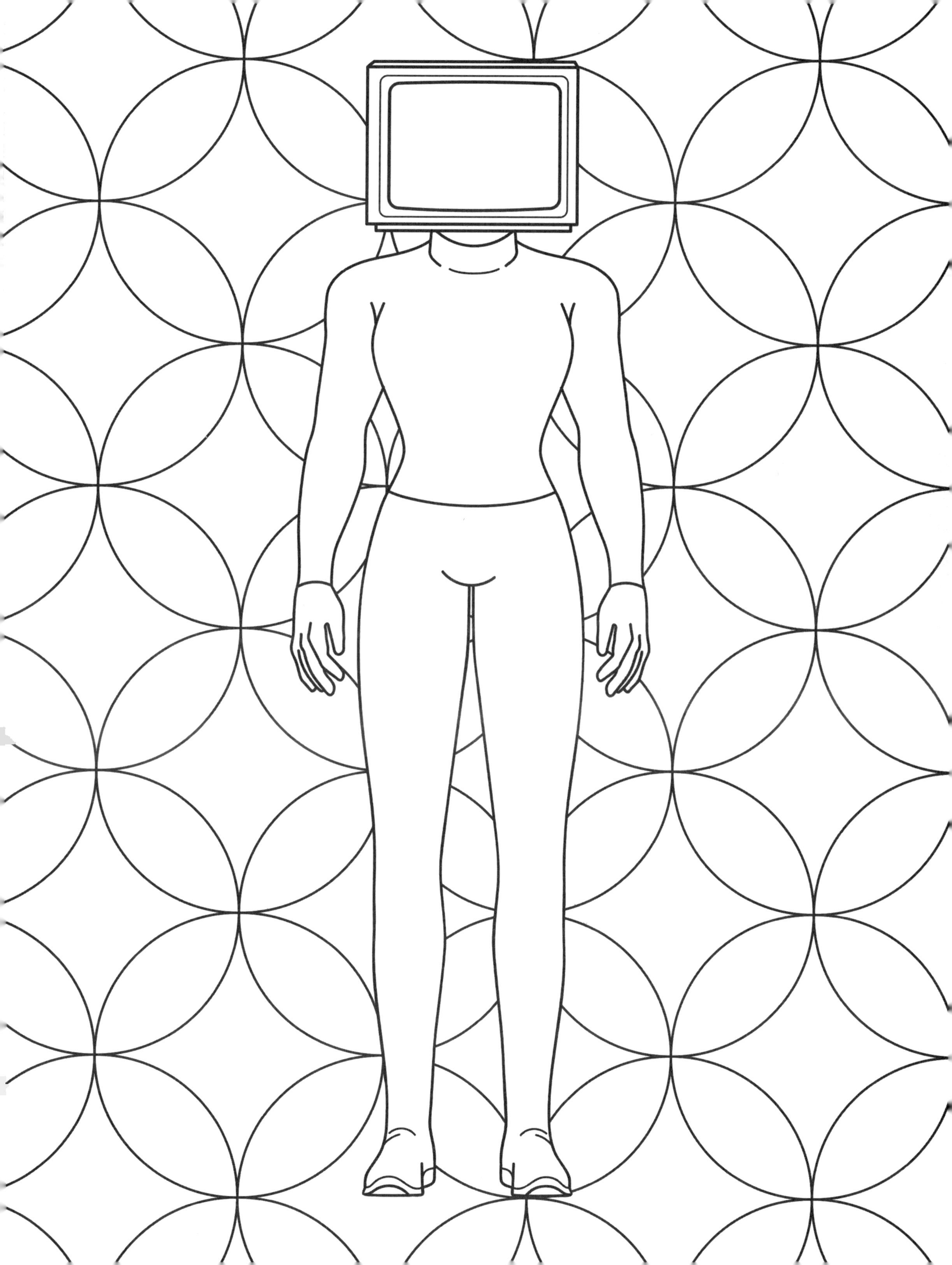

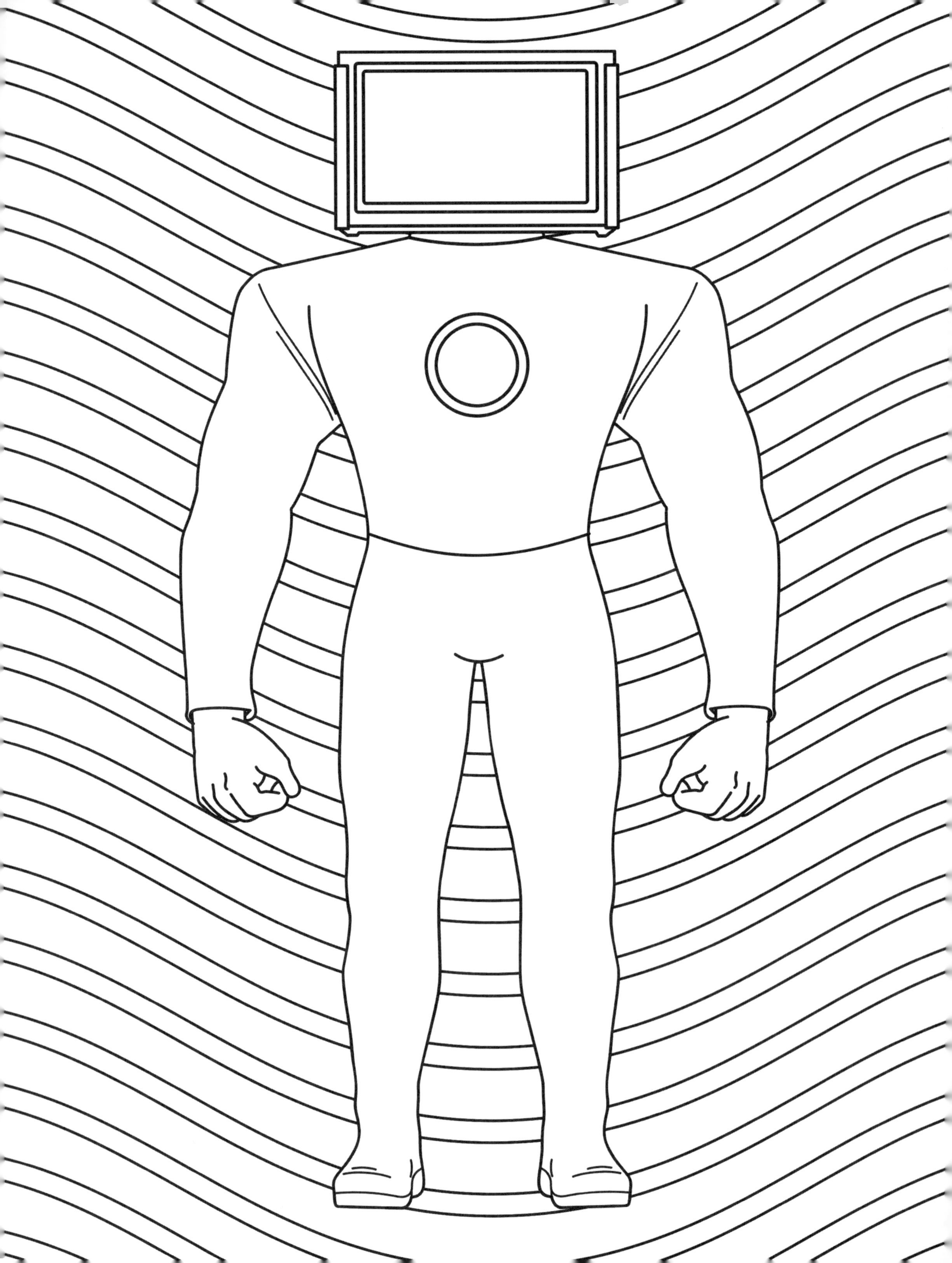

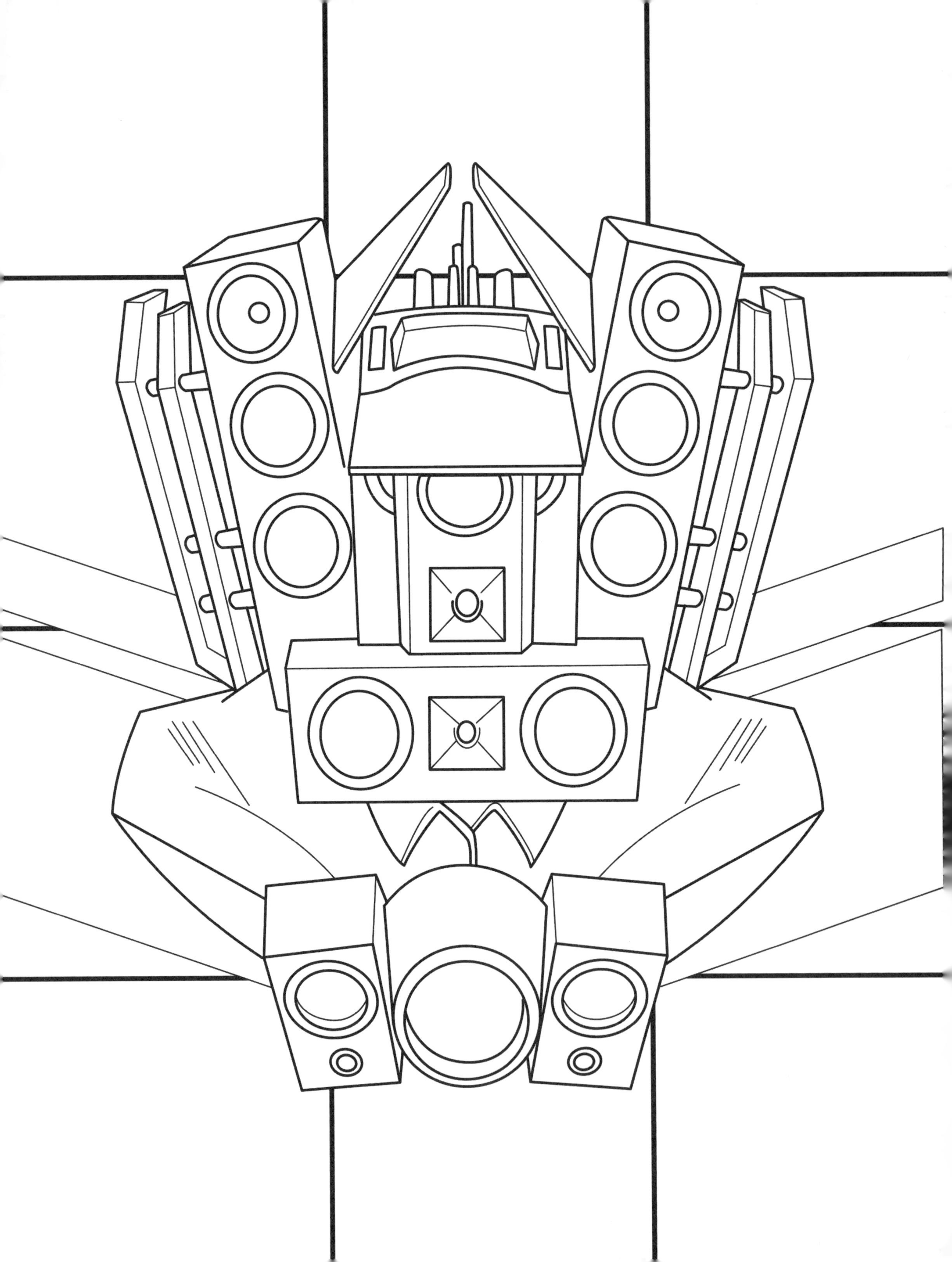

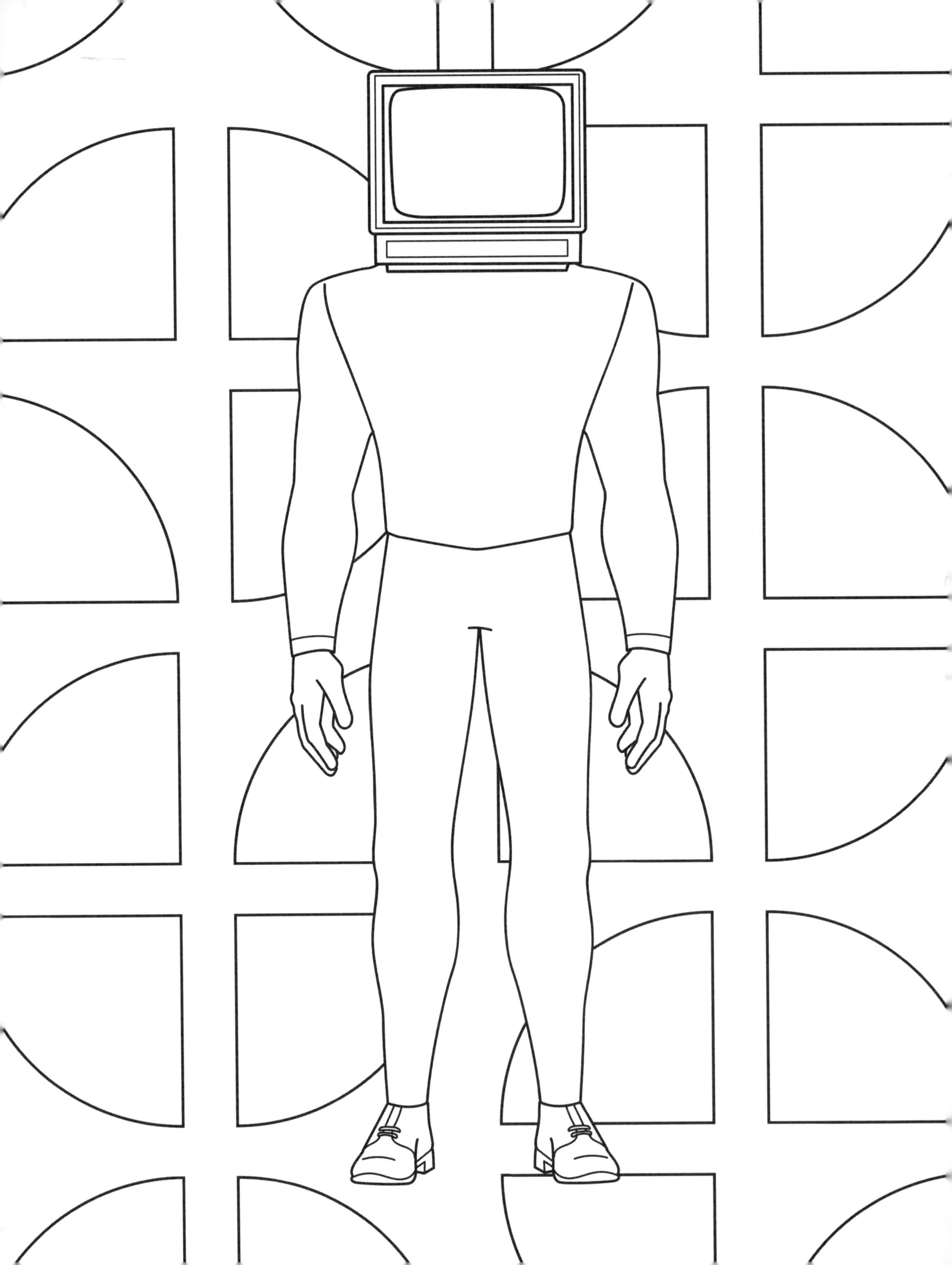

SKIBIDI
TOILET

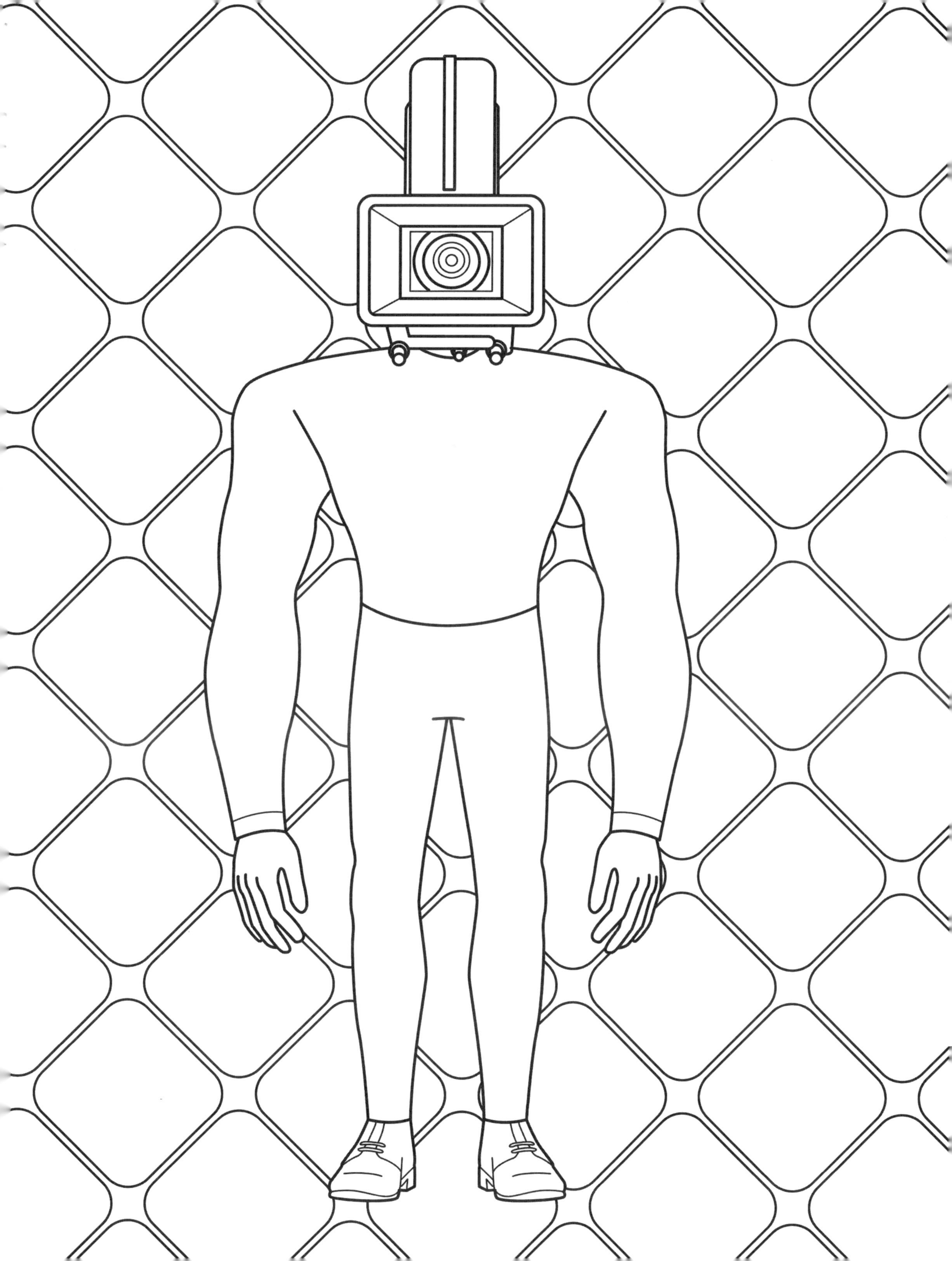

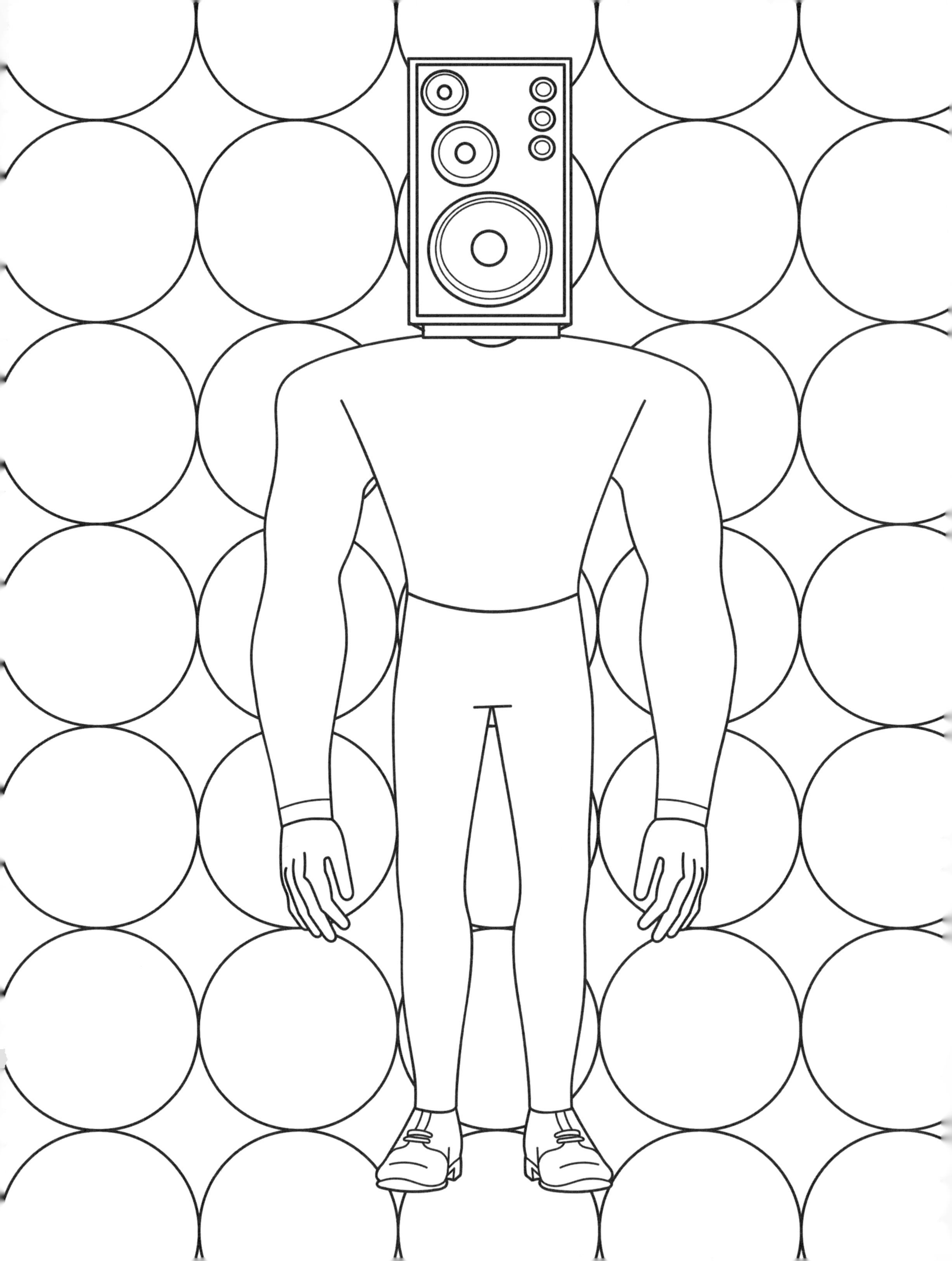

SKIBIDI
TOILET

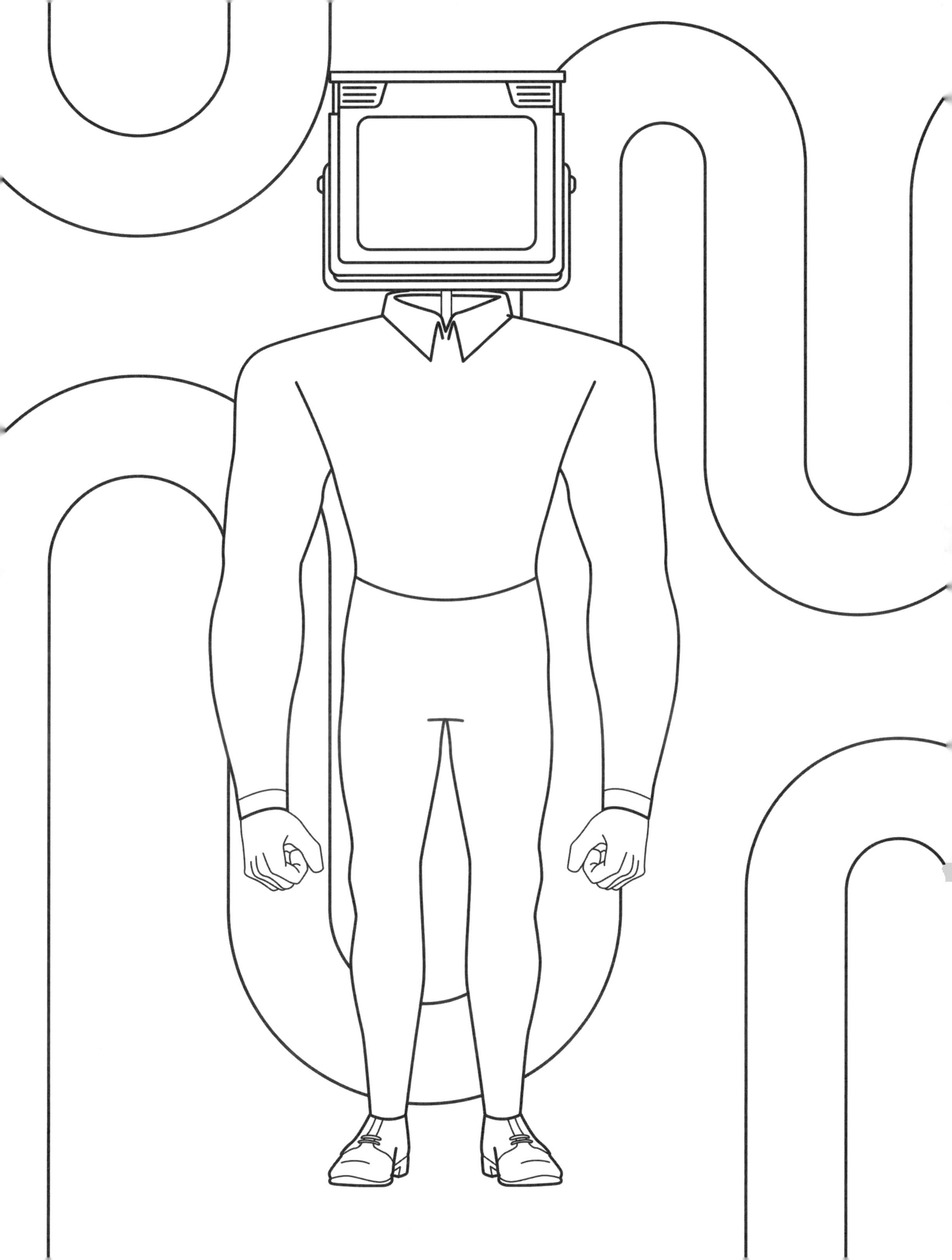

SKIBIDI
TOILET

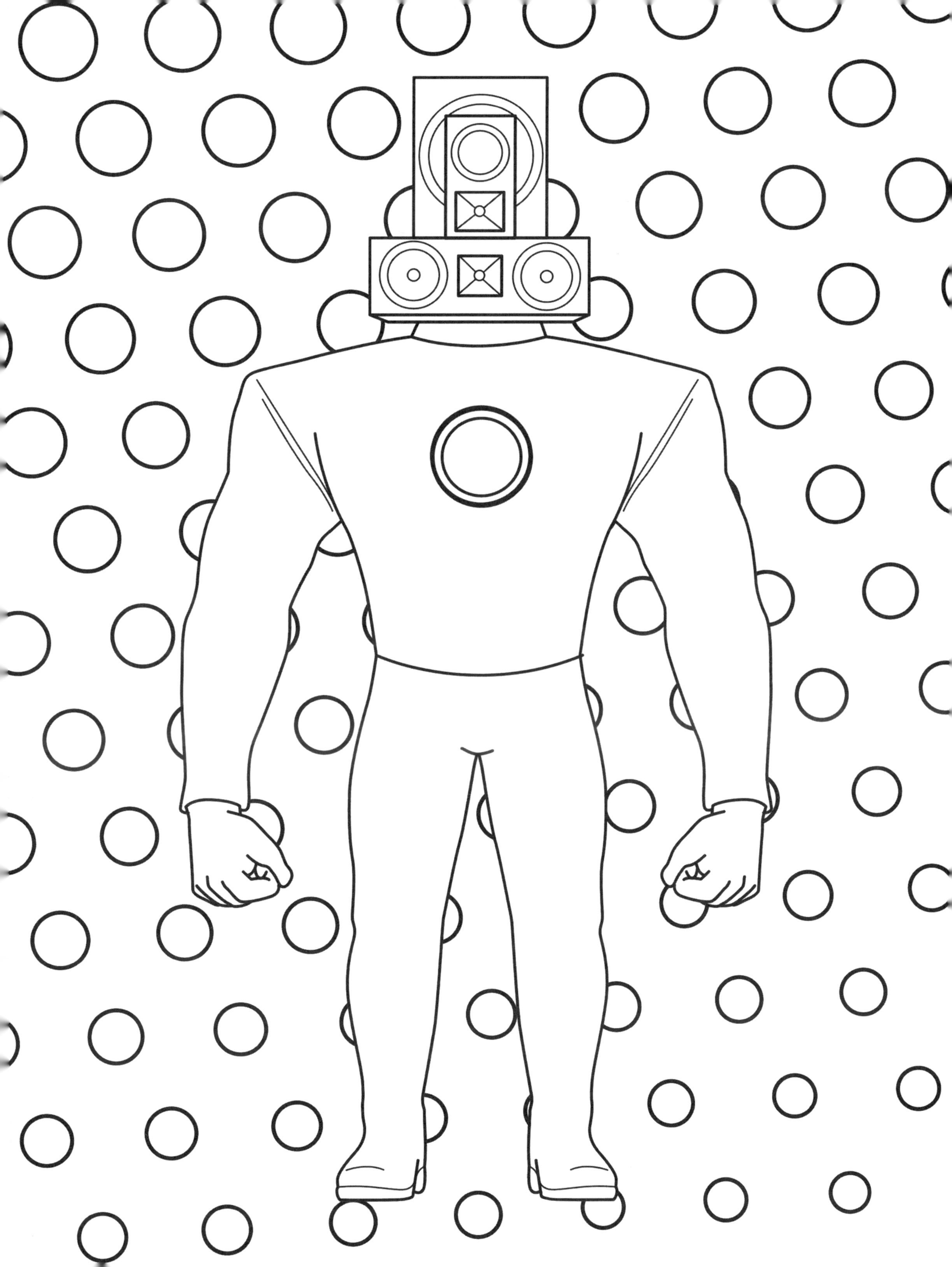

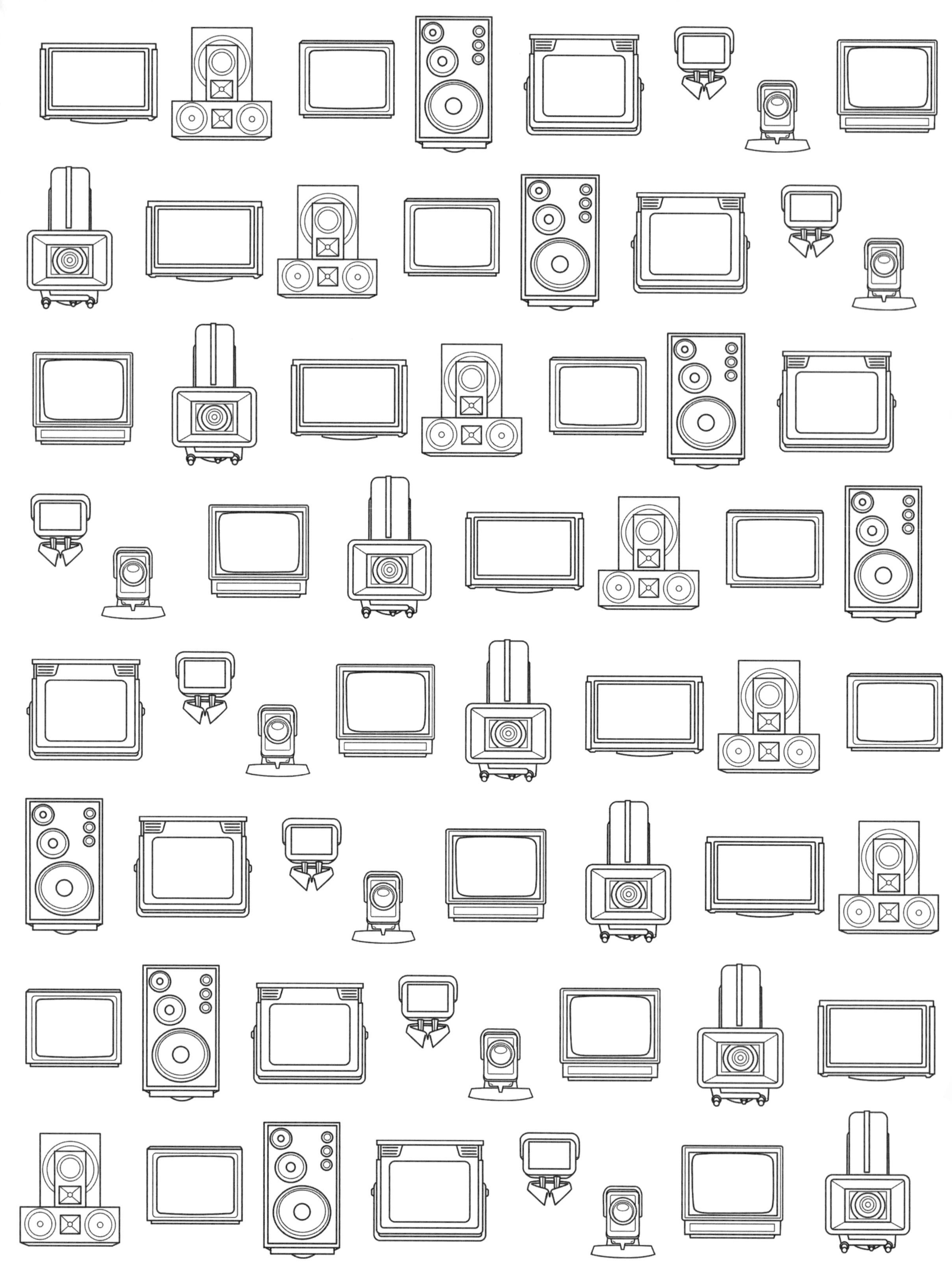

THWOOP!!